Izzy Beaver and The Bug Hotel

by

Mary Gonzalez

Illustrated by Geoffrey Cogan

Acknowledgements

Thanks to

Geoffrey Cogan

Joan Preston

Paul Naylor

For their help in composing the book

Preface

Izzy Beaver and his little friends have all made their homes on and around Brockie Field. Firstly, there's Izzy himself, who lives in his own little lodge, by the stream that runs through the field. Then there is Peggy Squirrel, who has her home in the trunk of a tree which stands in the middle of the field. There's Ron Raccoon who likes to think he's the leader of the 'gang,' his home is a very smart hut that he has built himself.

 There is Milly Mole, who is a timid little mole, and has to be encouraged by the others to join in their adventures.

In a treetop lives Olive Owl, she goes hunting every night for insects, with her friend Barney, who's a Bat, and Barney lives in Rectory Church belfry.

Harry Hedgehog likes to know everything that's going on, he's a very curious, or one could say 'nosey', little hedgehog. Lastly, there are the two little beavers, Molly and Betsy, their little lodge is next to Izzy Beaver's hut.

Mickey Ferret lives with his owners Lady Jane and the Squire, who in their kindness have bought for him a little, red, pedal car, in which he takes all his friends from the field on exciting trips. Their cottage is in a little country lane next to the field.

The little creatures get involved with Farmer Jones, whose farm is next to the field.

Daisy Cow lives on the farm, and she passes on all the news she hears of the goings on around and about, on to the little creatures.

They sometimes visit the Witch of the Woods in her cave, and have wonderful adventures going back in time. The witch has a Time Machine, which she made by putting a spell on a rickety old stool which she had standing in her cave.

IZZY BEAVER AND THE BUG HOTEL

CHAPTER ONE

Peggy Squirrel woke up to the sound of her

alarm clock ringing away. She leapt out of her

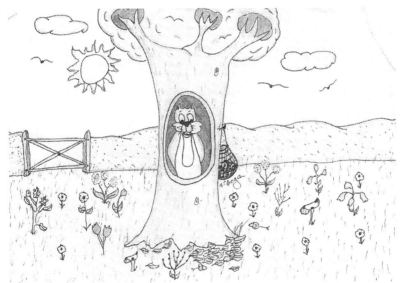

tiny bed and popped her head out of the door

of her little tree house. It was a beautiful day

in late summer, the sun was still warm and shining brightly, the fresh smell of grass and the wildflowers growing on Brockie Field filled her nostrils. 'Oh! What a lovely morning,' she said to herself, as she looked all around the field to see if any of the other creatures that lived there were up and about. There was no sign of anyone. 'I'll just skip off to the market,' she said to herself, 'To see what scraps I can gather for our breakfast.'

Peggy went to the market every morning to get food for herself and all the other little creatures living on the field.

There was Ron Raccoon, Izzy Beaver, Milly

Mole, Harry Hedgehog, Olive Owl, and the two

little beavers, Molly and Betsy.

Peggy picked up her basket and went

skipping down

the country

lanes heading   for

the local

market. On the

way, she

passed rows of neat little cottages with

gardens filled with late blooming summer

flowers; there were different colours and

shapes of dahlia, asters, great shrubs of

hydrangeas and tall sunflowers, some, very

tall indeed, with their heads stretching

upwards, seeming as though they were trying

to touch the sun; there was beautiful clematis

climbing around the cottage doors, and the

delicious smell of lilies wafted on the breeze

as she passed by. While in the hedgerows

there was still an array of wild flowers growing

in abundance, including cow parsley. Peggy

wondered if Daisy Cow ever ate or liked the

cow parsley; she thought she must remember

to ask her next time she saw her.

 Bumble bees flew from one flower to the next;

birds were singing happily in the trees,

knowing that their job for the year was over

and done, having hatched and raised their

fledglings, who now joined in the chorus,

singing from the tree tops.

In no time at all Peggy arrived at the

marketplace which was packed with people,

all busy shopping. She dodged, unnoticed, in

and out of the crowds, picking up lettuce

leaves and cabbage leaves, apples, oranges

and bananas and anything else that was good

to eat, which had fallen off the stalls.

Eventually, she came to the herb stall where

the owner, a kindly old lady, was busy filling

little paper bags with all different types of

herbs. As she packed the bags, some of the

herbs fell to the ground and Peggy, quick as a

flash, picked them up and popped them into

her basket.

'I already have some wild herbs, which I picked in the countryside, but these herbs will add much more flavour to my herb meals,' she thought to herself.

Meanwhile, the little creatures back at the field, were busy laying the table. Milly Mole had spread an old table cloth, which she kept hidden in one of her tunnels, over the table. (When the little creatures found anything useful on the field, left there by picnickers, they always kept them.) The table, itself, had been made by the little creatures, out of old railway sleepers would you believe, and they were very proud of it. Plates which had been

found by Ron Racoon, were placed, very

carefully upon it. Harry Hedgehog picked

some daisies, put them in a jam jar, which he

then placed in the middle of the table.

Soon Peggy Squirrel arrived back from the

market laden with goodies, and before long,

they were all tucking into a delicious breakfast.

'YUMMY!' they all agreed.

Suddenly, they realised that Izzy Beaver

wasn't with them. 'Oh, dear me!' said Olive

Owl, 'I forgot to do a roll call this morning and

hadn't realised that Izzy isn't here.'

'Oh dear! I do hope that old Grey Wolf hasn't

eaten him for dinner,' whispered a terrified

Milly Mole.

 Some years before, all the little creatures had lived in the nearby woods, but they'd been chased out by Grey Wolf; it was because of him they had had to make their homes on Brockie Field.

'O dear, let's hope not,' said Harry Hedgehog, with dread.

'I didn't hear any sounds coming from inside his lodge this morning,' said Molly Beaver.

'I usually see him dipping in the stream, but I didn't see him this morning,' piped up Betsy.

'Well, let's go and find him, we'll check inside his lodge first,' said Ron Racoon, so all the little creatures followed Ron to Izzy Beaver's lodge.

CHAPTER TWO

In no time at all they arrived at Izzy Beaver's lodge. 'Are you in there Izzy?' Ron Raccoon called out. There was no answer, so they all peeped inside and what did they see? and what did they hear? They could see him, and hear him, snoring loudly, still curled up on his little bed.

'Wake up lazy bones!' called Harry Hedgehog, loudly, but Izzy just carried on sleeping - and snoring!

'Oh dear, look at his face,' cried Milly Mole, who'd gone up to Izzy to give him a shake. 'It has red spots all over it.'

Just at that moment Izzy Beaver woke up with a start. 'What are you all doing in my lodge staring at me?' he cried, struggling to stand up. However, he wasn't very steady on his feet at all, and he fell backwards onto his bed.

'Well Izzy, seeing that you didn't arrive at the breakfast table this morning we came to find out why, and to see if there was anything wrong,' said Ron Raccoon.

I'm fine, I've just overslept,' said Izzy.

'No! you're not fine, your face is covered in spots and you were all wobbly when you stood up.' said Peggy Squirrel.

'My face, covered in spots, what nonsense,' cried Izzy. However, he stretched out and picked up a small, cracked mirror, which he kept at his bedside, and took a peep at

himself.

'Oh dear! you're right Peggy, and I do feel rather unsteady on my feet,' he said.

'Looks like you've caught a virus of some kind,' said Ron, 'So, in case it's catching, we'll stay outside and you must stay in bed 'til it goes.'

'Stay inside!' wailed Izzy, 'What will I do to pass the time?' I'll get so bored!'

'No you won't, I'll bring you some toys and paper and paints so you'll have something to occupy your time with.' 'Lady Jane has a basket full of toys which she keeps for visiting children to play with, I'll borrow some of them for you,' said Mickey Ferret.

'That's a good idea for you Izzy, you've always wanted to paint.' 'Now you'll be able to, and when you're better you can display all your drawings outside your lodge so everyone can see what you've been doing,' said Harry Hedgehog.

With that, Mickey Ferret raced off home in his little red car before Izzy could say anything else.

'I'll go home and make some medicine with the fresh herbs I brought home from the market this morning,' announced Peggy Squirrel. 'I've got thyme, basil, ginger and bay leaves, I'll boil them all together and bring the mixture for you to drink.'

'Ugh!' 'It will probably taste horrible,'
complained Izzy. 'No it won't, I've got some
honey that you can take with it,' said Molly
Beaver. 'And I've got some liquorice sweets
that I'll give you, you   can suck on them." said
Betsy Beaver. Milly Mole told Izzy not to
worry, as she would leave some breakfast
outside his lodge every morning until he was
better. With that, all the little creatures
scurried away to collect anything they could
that would help Izzy Beaver feel a little better.

CHAPTER THREE

When Mickey Ferret reached his cottage, he squeezed in through the cat flap.

Once inside he could hear Lady Jane reading from the newspaper out loud to the Squire. 'It says in today's paper that Chickenpox is going around,' she said. 'I caught it when I was a child, so I can't catch it again, which means,

that I can happily go out and about as usual, in

fact, I'm going out right now to see if Farmer

Jones needs any help in the farm shop,' with

that she let herself out through the front door.

The Squire also went out, but he only went as

far as his shed to 'tinker about' - pretending to

be doing some work.

Mickey Ferret lost no time, he quickly put a

skipping rope, a drawing pad, some paints and

 a jigsaw puzzle
into a plastic bag.
The toy box was
full of toys as he'd
said, but Mickey
thought he'd put

enough things in the bag to keep Izzy busy.

When he left the cottage, the Squire had gone

out through the back door leaving it wide

open, so Mickey scurried out through this

carrying the bag, which may have got stuck if

he'd used the cat flap as he had on his way

into the cottage.

He loaded up his little red pedal car that Lady

Jane and the Squire had bought him; and

which he used to take all his little friends on

the filed out and about in. He then drove, as

fast as he could, back to Brockie Field.

Back at home, in the old oak tree, Peggy

Squirrel opened her cupboard door in the

kitchen and took out a wooden bowl, called a

mortar, which is used together with something

called a pestle, (these items are used

especially for crushing herbs.) She then placed some of the herbs, the garlic, basil, bay leaves and a pinch of ginger, which she'd already boiled and drained, into the mortar, then she pounded them with the pestle; she added a teaspoon of olive oil then filled the mortar with the drained water from the herbs. 'Mission accomplished!' she said to herself, as she took a cup from a shelf and hurried back to Izzy Beaver's lodge, carefully carrying the mixture she'd made.

At the same time that Peggy arrived at Izzy Beaver's lodge, Molly arrived carrying her pot of honey.

'Helloooo there, Izzy! called out Peggy, 'We can't come inside in case

 we catch the virus that you might have, so here we are at the doorway with the medicine and honey,'

Izzy Beaver was still lying on his bed feeling rather sorry for himself, he didn't feel up to seeing visitors. 'Go away!' he called out, 'I just want to sleep.'

'We only want to help you,' Peggy said, 'If you don't take the medicine then you won't get better.' 'The sooner you take it, the sooner you'll be able to come out and about with us again.'

Izzy slowly got up and went to the doorway, he picked up the cup of medicine that Peggy had placed there for him. 'I'm not sure about drinking this,' he said, as he peered suspiciously into the cup.

Suddenly Ron Raccoon also appeared at the doorway. 'Come on, Izzy, drink up,' he said, giving Izzy a stern look, 'We're only trying to help you.'

All the little creatures did as they were told by Ron Raccoon because he was their leader, so Izzy, meekly, took the cup from Peggy. 'It's not too bad, but where's the honey?' said Izzy, as he quickly drank the liquid.

'Here you are, fresh honey,' said Molly

Beaver, passing Izzy the jar. Izzy quickly

swallowed some of the honey. 'Well, that

wasn't too bad, the honey made it go down

better, thank you Peggy and thank you Molly '

said Izzy Beaver. 'Do you know, I think I'm

feeling better already, so can I come out with

you today?'

'No you can't!' said Ron Racoon sternly. 'You can't have gotten better so soon, you've only just taken the medicine.'

'Well, I'm so bored on my own,' wailed Izzy, pulling a sad face.

Just at that moment Mickey Ferret arrived with the bag of 'goodies' and immediately Izzy cheered up when he spotted what was inside the bag.

'A skipping rope, I love skipping, oh, and some

paints and brushes and paper, Harry

Hedgehog was right when he said that I've

always wanted to paint.' said Izzy, excitedly.

"What else have you brought for me Mickey?'

A jigsaw puzzle, I can see a jigsaw puzzle, I

love jigsaw puzzles as well,' he said, as

Mickey placed the bag and its contents inside Izzy's doorway.

While Izzy was busy sorting through the things Mickey had brought, Mickey himself, drove all the friends, in his little red car, to the Three Sisters Recreational Centre, a place where they could play in safety, all day long.

CHAPTER FOUR

When the little creatures arrived at the 'Three

Sisters,' they headed straight for the play area.

Harry Hedgehog played in the sand pit while

the others took turns on the slide and the

swings.

At first, there was no-one else around but

then, as a Ranger appeared in the doorway of

the cafe, which was next to the lake where the

Ranger would feed the swans, a crowd of

people arrived and the little creatures heard

the Ranger saying, 'Hello and welcome!'

'You're the first to arrive for the guided tour,

during which I'll show you the latest project

we're working on, it's called a Bug Hotel, but

before we get underway, please excuse me,

I'll be with you in just two ticks.' he said, as he disappeared back inside the cafe.

'Did you hear that?' said Ron Raccoon, 'He's getting ready to take those people on a tour of the grounds.' 'We could follow them, and as there's a lot of people they won't notice us'.

So, as everyone walked along the reserve trail the little creatures followed behind them, unnoticed, just as Ron had said.

The Ranger pointed out places of interest as

they walked along under the tall, shady trees.

'Listen!' 'Can you hear the whirring of the

wings of the

dragonflies,'

he said,

pointing to a

cloud of them

buzzing

around. 'Just

look at them performing their aerobatics,

twisting and zooming, up and down,

backwards and forwards, 'round and around.'

'We see plenty of dragonflies in the evenings on Brockie Field,' whispered Betsy Beaver to Molly Beaver. 'Yes we do, they fly above, and all around the stream, because they like shaded ponds and water.' whispered Peggy Squirrel.

'Did someone say something?' asked the Ranger, stopping and turning around.

Everyone shook their heads, nobody had noticed the little animals following along because they had been far too interested in what the Ranger had had to say.

Dragonflies are important to humans, as they kill mosquitos and other midges helping to keep their numbers in check.

'We make new ponds for them like this one here,' said the Ranger. 'You see, there are no fish in it - fish would eat them - and they like the shade, so they gather here; all our nature reserves are important to the dragonflies,' he said, as he turned and marched on along the pathway.

Little rabbits scurried out of the way as the party walked along, and they could hear the birds as they sang in the treetops.

Quite suddenly, the Ranger stopped beside

several, small wooden constructions which

had a sign hanging on each of one of them.

'Can you read what those signs say?' he

asked the children in the group. 'It says Bug

Hotel,' chorused the children. 'That's right,

and in these hotels, that's just what we keep -

bugs!' said the Ranger.

'What kind of bugs?' asked one little girl.

'Why do you want to keep bugs there anyway?' asked another.

'Well,' said the Ranger, 'The answer to the first question is - the bugs that live here are lacewings, ladybugs, beetles, earwigs, wasps, bees plus many others, of course.' 'And the answer to the second question, why do we keep bugs here? Is that bugs and insects are very important.' 'Apart from anything else, they will attract all kinds of birds to the area and so then we will have many more different kinds of birds to spot, we'll also get grass snakes, frogs and toads.

'You can make bug hotels for your gardens,' said the Ranger to the adults, 'It's not difficult, why don't you give it a try, I'm sure your children would love to help.'

It was at this point that Ron Raccoon decided it was time to go back home. 'We can't leave Izzy Beaver too long on his own,' he whispered, and the little creatures all made

their way back to Mickey Ferret's little red car.

CHAPTER FIVE

When the little creatures arrived back at

Brockie Field they went to Izzy's and quietly,

peeping inside, they saw that he was fast

asleep. 'My medicine has made him sleepy,'

said Peggy Squirrel.

'Let's all hope that it makes him better soon,' said Milly Mole. 'I'll keep bringing Peggy's Medicine and Molly's honey with his breakfast each morning, as I promised I would, and leave it outside his lodge for him to pick up.' And with that they all went, feeling rather sad, to their own little homes which were dotted around the field.

Usually, each evening, they would have a storytelling session, when they would sit on a bench, which they had made themselves and had placed it in the far corner of the field, and now that corner was called - The Storytelling

Corner, -- but nobody felt like going there tonight, not without Izzy Beaver.

A week went by and Izzy improved a little each day and although he hated the taste of his medicine he swallowed it, followed quickly by the honey. In the second week, the little creatures saw, to their surprise, Izzy doing somersaults outside his lodge.

'My

spots have all gone, I'm all better, YIPPEE!,'

he called out. ' I feel so good, and look at what

I've done.' They looked around, and to their

surprise, they saw that Izzy had taken every

painting he'd done and spread them all across

the bench in the Storytelling Corner.

'Wow! Izzy, we can see that you've been very

busy painting, just look at all those lovely

pictures you've created, there's

pictures of ducks, geese, cows, and beautiful

wildflowers; you've even painted pictures of

your little friends from here on Brockie Field,'

said Ron Racoon, 'And, by the look of things,

you're back to being your old self.' 'Yes,

thanks to Peggy Squirrel's medicine I'm

feeling fine,' said Izzy Beaver.

Just at that moment, Olive Owl flew down from

her nest in the oak tree, which was in the

middle of the field. 'I'm glad to see your spots

have all gone,' she said to Izzy; who did

another somersault to prove to Olive and, to

everyone else, that he was completely better,

and to show just how good he felt, and also -

just to show off!

Suddenly, Daisy Cow, who lived on Farmer Jones' field, popped her head over the hedge which ran alongside Brockie Field.

Daisy was the one who got to hear, and spread, all the news of things happening on the farm, in the local woods and all around the area. This was because the little birds which came into Daisy's shed and perched in the rafters, while they watched her being milked, told her all about what they'd seen, or heard, while on their travels.

'Hello there,' said Daisy. 'I've come to see how you are Izzy Beaver.' 'My bird friends told me that you had Chickenpox but I can see that you're better now.'

Stretching her neck further over the hedge she said, 'Ohhhh! I do like that painting of the cows, can I have it for my cowshed?'

Izzy thought for a while, but he didn't really like parting with things so he said, 'Sorry!' 'No!' 'I want it for my lodge.'

'Well, never mind, I've got some news which I will tell you, if you let me have a mint ball,' said Daisy. 'Sorry I haven't got any mint balls today,' said Mickey Ferret who usually had a pocket full. 'Lady Jane wouldn't let me have any today,' he explained.' 'She says I eat too many.' What Lady Jane didn't know was that Mickey gave some of the mint balls to Daisy Cow, in exchange   for information from her.

'Right! let me have that painting then,' said Daisy.

'Oh, go on, give it to her, you know how we all like to hear what news Daisy has to tell of the goings on around here,' said Harry Hedgehog, who was, as usual, being a very curious - or should we say - nosey - little hedgehog.

 Izzy thought for a moment, then said very reluctantly, 'I suppose I don't really need a picture of cows in my lodge, and besides, I have plenty of other drawings.'

'Okay, Daisy,' he finally said, 'You can have it.'

'Thank you Izzy, I'll take it when I'm leaving.'

'Now for my news, it's this - Farmer Jones isn't well.' 'It seems that because he did have Chickenpox when he was a child, and because it's going around again, he's got something called Shingles. Shingles is something grown-ups can get if they had Chickenpox when they were young.'

'He has a very bad rash, and it's catching,' she went on, 'Tommy Tinker has had to take over the running of the farm until he's better.'

'His wife is nursing him,' she continued, 'and

Lady Jane is helping them out by running the farm shop.' She finished by telling them that most of the village children now had the Chickenpox.

'I can tell you something else you don't know, but you'll have to give me another painting,' said Daisy craftily.

'Just one more then,' said Izzy Beaver, who was actually quite flattered that Daisy Cow liked his paintings so much.

'Well now, did you know, that it's thanks to cows like me that there is such a thing called a vaccine, which is a type of medicine that can make you immune and safe when used against Chickenpox and other diseases?' said Daisy Cow. As she said this, all the little creatures fell about laughing. 'Ha! ha! ha! aren't you being rather big-headed Daisy,' said Ron Raccoon.

'No I am not!' said Daisy angrily. 'Years ago, one man realized that the maids that milked the cows and caught Cowpox never caught Smallpox, which was a

deadly disease at that time, most people who caught it - died.'

'So,' said Daisy, still sounding just a little annoyed, 'That does mean that cows must have had something special.'

'She's right,' said wise Olive Owl, 'I know all about it.' 'You all know that I learned how to read when I was young, and when you can read you find out all sorts of interesting things.' 'Well, I once read an article, in a discarded magazine, which I had found in a ditch, about a man named Doctor Edward Jenner who, almost three hundred years ago, was responsible for the discovery of how to make the special type of medicine, called a vaccine, which helped people get better from Smallpox.' 'He did this from what he had learned about the milkmaids and their Cowpox which then, in turn, led to how other vaccines were discovered that would cure Chickenpox among other diseases.' 'So!', she continued, 'There you have it - there was the vaccine, there was the Doctor who studied the maids from the milking parlours, and before them, there were the cows, so you see, cows were an important part of the story.'

'Now I must go, and catch up on my daytime sleep,' said Olive, 'As tonight, I'll be busy flying around the woods, as usual, with Barney Bat,

looking for mice and insects,' and with that,

away she flew.

'What a great story,' said Izzy Beaver. 'And

it's all true, ' said Daisy, proudly.

So Izzy, willingly, gave Daisy Cow the

paintings she'd asked for, she grasped them in

her mouth and then ambled contentedly, back

to her cowshed.

CHAPTER SIX

The next morning Izzy Beaver woke up early.

The sun was shining brightly into his little

lodge and he felt happy because he felt so

well. 'I'll go for a dip in the stream before

breakfast,' he thought to himself.

When he arrived at the stream he dived in and

then noticed that Molly and Betsy Beaver were

already splashing around. 'Glad to see you

back from your isolation in your lodge,' said Molly. 'Yes, I'm glad that you're better, as well,' said Betsy.

'Did I miss out on anything?' Did anything interesting happen while I was ill?' 'Did you go on any trips in Mickey Ferret's car?' Izzy fired the questions at them. He didn't like to think he'd missed out on anything.

'Well, yes, we did go on a trip, we went to the Three Sisters Recreational Centre and we saw something called Bug Hotels,' said Molly.

'Bug Hotels, I've never heard of such things, what are they?' asked Izzy Beaver, puzzled.

Molly and Betsy told Izzy all about what they'd overheard the Ranger telling a group of people, as he was showing them around the nature reserve, all about what a Bug Hotel was for, and how easy it would be to make one.

Just at that moment they heard a bell ringing. 'That will be Peggy Squirrel ringing her little handbell to make sure we all turn up for breakfast.' said Betsy Beaver and straight away, the three beavers ran off to join the others at the breakfast table.

Harry Hedgehog was already there, he was

always punctual, he so hated to miss out on

anything that went on.

 The rest of the little creatures, all except

Mickey Ferret, arrived together, just as Peggy

Squirrel was placing a stack of fruit and nuts

on the table. Olive Owl flew down from her

tree and landed on the table.

'Before we make a start, I'll do a roll call,' she said, 'Just to make sure that nobody is missing with the Chickenpox again.'

''Milly Mole,' called Olive.

'Here,' said Milly.

'Betsy and Molly Beaver,' called Olive.

'We're both here.' answered Molly

Harry Hedgehog's name is called next.

'I'm here, I was the first,' said Harry.

Ron Raccoon,' called Olive.

'I'm here as usual,' replied Ron.

'Peggy Squirrel,' called Olive.

'Of course, I'm here Olive, you can see I'm here' said Peggy. 'There'd be no breakfast for you all if I weren't here.'

Next, Olive called out, - 'Mickey Ferret!' There was no reply.

'Mickey Ferret!' she called again, sharply.

There was only silence. There was no sign of Mickey Ferret.

'I wonder where he can be,' said Harry Hedgehog 'Maybe he's caught the Chickenpox,' said Ron Raccoon.

'Well, if that's the case, I'm here, and I've got plenty of medicine and honey left.' said Peggy Squirrel. 'That's a good thing Peggy,' said

Izzy. 'Your medicine, and Molly's honey,

certainly made me better,'

Just then, they could hear Mickey Ferret's car,

he was tooting the horn as he drove it onto the

field.

'Sorry I'm late, but guess what?' he said,

rushing over to the friends. 'What?' 'What?'

asked the ever curious Harry Hedgehog.

'What!.' 'What is it?' 'Oh do tell us, 'he pleaded.

Mickey Ferret was very pleased that he had

everyone's attention, and said, feeling rather

important. 'Sorry, you'll have to wait.' 'I'll tell

you the news after breakfast, even though I've

already had some ferret food I'd still love one

of those lovely, rosy apples,' he said, helping

himself.

As they were now all 'present and correct' the little creatures tucked into their breakfast. As soon as it was over Harry Hedgehog said eagerly, 'Now are you going to tell us what's going on?'

Mickey made sure they were all listening, then he began. 'Lady Jane and the Squire have just built a Bug Hotel at the bottom of their garden.' said Mickey, 'The Squire had some wooden pallets which he didn't know what to do with, so he decided to use them to make a Bug Hotel, and that gave me ever such a good idea,' he added.

'What idea?' asked Ron Raccoon, feeling a little jealous, because he liked to be the one to come up with ideas for projects for the little creatures to work on.

'Why don't we build our own Bug Hotel next to the Storytelling Corner?' said Mickey.

'Build a Bug Hotel, what materials would we need, and where would we get them from?' asked Ron.

'That's easy,' said Mickey. 'I can get the wooden pallets we need, the Squire has some stashed away in his work shed.' 'I'll also borrow some of his tools, along with a hand saw, which we can then use to saw the wood to the sizes we need.'

'Right then,' said Ron. 'We'll need to collect plenty of dry leaves, twigs, bits of bark, pine cones, hollow stems like bamboo cane, bits of straw, not forgetting some soft materials, such as moss, in fact, all the items we overheard the Ranger mention when we were at the 'Three Sisters.'

'I'll go to the woods and collect the leaves and bits of bark,' said Izzy Beaver, eager to help.

'I'll go to Farmer Jones' farm for bits of straw,' said Betsy Beaver. 'I'll go with you,' chipped in Molly.

Not to be out done Milly Mole said she would go on a 'scavenger hunt' to see what she could find that would be of use, maybe bits of broken terracotta plant pots, she knew that plastic pots would be of no use, and if she was really lucky she might find bits of felt, after all the bug hotel would need a roof.

'Well then, let's get organised,' said Ron. 'You and I will build the hotel Mickey, and you, Harry Hedgehog, can be in charge of handing out the tools,' At this Mickey Ferret

raced off home to get the tools and pallets

while the others all hurried off to find whatever

they could.

CHAPTER SEVEN

It was evening when the little friends arrived back on Brockie Field. By this time, Ron Raccoon and Mickey Ferret, with the help of Harry Hedgehog, had built the Bug Hotel.

They'd drilled holes in the wood; they'd made separate compartments inside and made sure the roof was pointed so rain would run off. The little friends then stuffed in the bits of bark, pine cones, clumps of moss, pieces of straw, cardboard and even a few bits of broken pots that Milly Mole had found. Izzy Beaver then ran off to his lodge to fetch the paints which Mickey Ferret had given him

when he was confined to his lodge with the

Chickenpox. When he got back, he handed

them to Olive Owl, who could read and write,

so she could paint the words 'Bug Hotel' on it.

When they'd finished, they all stood back to

admire their handy work.

'Well done all of you,' they heard a voice say.

'Who said that?' asked Ron Racoon. 'Who

spoke?'

They all turned round but couldn't see anyone.

Suddenly Daisy Cow popped her head over

the hedge. 'It was me, I'm the one who spoke,'

she said.

'I was just congratulating you, that hotel looks
very smart, all ready for tenants to move in
when Autumn arrives.' 'If it was bigger, I'd be
tempted to stay in it myself.' 'Are you taking
bookings?'

'It happens to be for bugs only,' said Harry
Hedgehog.

'Well then, you'll have to go and find the insects to live in it when the time comes,' said Daisy.

'No we won't,' Mickey told her. 'We've done the hard work building them an hotel.' 'It's up to the bugs to make themselves at home.' 'We expect ladybirds to arrive and be happy with the rooms of dry leaves, sticks and straw.' 'Spiders and beetles will 'book' into the room of dried wood and bark.' 'Single bees will enjoy the small tubes and hollow bamboo.' he went on. 'Centipedes and other 'crawlies' will love the snug holes that Ron and I have drilled.' 'The corrugated cardboard is ideal for lacewings and maybe, a toad may find its way and 'live' in the centre, among the stones and bits of broken pots, where it will be protected from frost in the winter.' 'And,' he went on, 'Who knows, we could even end up with a new friend. We've put it in the Storytelling Corner where it will be sheltered from the bad winter weather and frost.

Just then, Daisy said she had some news to share, at a price, of course.

'Oh do tell us what you know,' said Harry Hedgehog.

'You know the price for telling, I'll need a mint ball,' said Daisy.

Mickey Ferret was in a good mood as Lady

Jane had filled his pockets with mint balls

when he'd gone to fetch the pallets, and he

was also pleased with Daisy Cow because

she had congratulated him, so he tossed her a

mint ball. 'Come on now Daisy, tell us what it

is that you know, ' repeated Harry Hedgehog.

Daisy chewed the mint slowly, then asked for another. 'Don't be so greedy Daisy and tell us what you have to say,' said Ron Raccoon sternly. Daisy was disappointed, but she told them her news anyway.

'A blackbird flew into my cow shed this morning and told me that the Witch of the Woods is unwell.'

The Witch of the Woods lived with her cat, Trixie, in a cave deep in the woods. This cave was well hidden from view, behind a 'curtain' of Ivy which grew over the entrance. Nobody knew she lived there, except the little creatures, Daisy Cow and the birds of the wood.

'The witch - ill, she can't be.' 'She's never ill, at least we've never known her to be ill, and we've known her a long time,' said Izzy Beaver. 'Oh dear, how sad, I hope she gets better soon, I'll let her have some of my honey,' said Molly who was also very nervous of the witch, but she was a kind hearted little beaver and felt sorry for her, because she knew that the witch had only her cat for a friend.

'Well at least she's never cast a spell on us,' said Ron Racoon, "So I think we should help her.' ''Yes, we should, she can definitely have some of my medicine,' said Peggy Squirrel. 'Do you all remember the time she sent us to Ancient Egypt in her Time Machine?' said Betsy Beaver.

The witch had once cast a spell over her stool and it had become a Time Machine. 'Yes, maybe if we help her get better, she'll lend it to us again,' said Harry Hedgehog, hopefully. 'Oh, yes, that would be wonderful, maybe we could go back to Ancient Greece next time, or, maybe to the days of Cavemen and Dinosaurs,' said Betsy Beaver, wistfully, imagining such an adventure.

'Let's not waste any more time chatting, we need to go to her now,' said Ron in his best organising voice.

''I'll take you all in my little car ' Mickey said, "It's full of the Squires tools at the moment, but I'll drop them off home and then come back and pick you up in just a little while.'

With that he drove off to his cottage leaving the others waiting for him to return.

CHAPTER EIGHT

Mickey Ferret drove along the narrow, deserted, country lane. As he drove, he couldn't help but admire the wonderful display of wild flowers lining each side of the lane. Among others there were bluebells, white daisies, purple orchids, violets, primroses and tall cow parsley, and Mickey could see bees,

buzzing in and out of each one, pollinating

them as they went about their business. He

arrived at his owners' cottage and pulled up

outside and quickly took the tools from his car

and returned them to the shed in the back

garden. He passed the bug hotel that the

Squire and Lady Jane had made, and peeped

inside. 'Oh it looks so good, I can't wait for the

insects to arrive later in the year and for the

hotel to have a 'no vacancies,' sign hanging

outside.' said Mickey contentedly to himself.

Then he jumped back into his little red car and

drove away to pick up his friends at the field.

The little creatures were still waiting where

he'd left them, they all climbed into the car and

drove off. On their way to the woods they

passed Farmer Jones' field where they saw

Daisy standing at the gate, 'Hey there,' she

called. 'Come here, I have more news for

you.'

'Sorry! we're too busy, we're on our way to the

woods to visit the witch,' called Ron Raccoon.

'Well she's what I wanted to tell you about,'

called Daisy, 'According to my informant, the black bird, she's in a foul mood.' 'You'd better watch out.' 'When she's in one of those moods she might put a spell on you, maybe turn you all into field mice.' Milly Mole was terrified, 'I don't think I'll go any further, maybe you could let me out just here,' she cried.

'Milly, where's your sense of adventure?' asked Peggy Squirrel.

Milly Mole hesitated, then she remembered that she had the honey with her to give to the witch. 'Ok,' she said, rather reluctantly, 'I'll carry on with you.'

'Good for you Milly Mole,' said Ron Raccoon; and Mickey Ferret, who had just been about to put the brakes on, carried on pedalling furiously.

They arrived at the woods, and as Mickey drove the car along the narrow footpaths, rabbits and hares leapt out of the way, and as he continued to drive along, they could hear

birds singing in the tall oaks and beech trees,

and there were butterflies flying everywhere;

soon they arrived outside the witch's cave.

CHAPTER NINE

The little creatures climbed out of the car and peeped into the cave. They could see the witch peering at herself in a mirror which was hanging on one of the walls.

The cave looked the same as it always did, with photos of the witch's ancestors hanging from nails on every wall. Trixie the cat was asleep in her basket, and a cauldron of

soup, hanging from a hook, simmered over a

log fire in a corner.

'Oh, just look at me, I've got spots all over

me, even on my beautiful face.' she wailed,

then she spotted the little creatures reflected

in her mirror and she spun around.

'What are you doing here?' she cried, 'Why

are you all staring into my cave?'

'We've come on a mission,' said Ron Raccoon

as usual taking charge of the situation.

'Mission?' 'Are you sure you're not out to make

mischief?' cried the witch. 'If so I'll conjure up

a spell and turn you all into field mice.'

'I knew she would do that, I said she would,

oh! I knew I shouldn't have come,' whimpered

Milly Mole. 'Be quiet Milly, we have to be nice

to her, we all know she has a quick temper but

it soon dies down, so hush, you know we all

want another trip in her Time Machine,'

whispered Izzy Beaver.

'Time Machine, I heard you, you said Time

Machine,' croaked the witch. 'If you're after

another trip in my Time Machine, then I'm sorry to have to disappoint you, it won't work, it's out of order.' 'I tried to turn it back into a stool, which it used to be - you see, I'm a little short of stools here, however, the spell went wrong and now, I've no stool, and a machine that won't work.'

'Never mind all that, we heard that you weren't well,' interrupted Ron Racoon. 'And we've all come to help you get better.' ' You see, when Izzy Beaver had Chickenpox, and it does look as though you have it now, he was cured with a mixture of Peggy Squirrel's medicine and Molly Beaver's honey.' 'If we give it to you, and you take it every day, you'll get better in no time at all.'

'That's most thoughtful of you,' said the witch, 'I will then be in debt to you each one of you for your kindness and good deed.'

'When I'm fully better, I'll have to make a trip to Transylvania to meet up with some friends of mine, a coven of good witches, and, with a bit of luck they'll be able to help me find the right spell to fix my Time Machine.'

'Until then,' she said, 'You will all have to be patient, but here, take this toad I was going to make soup with it, but you can have it in exchange for Peggy Squirrel's medicine and

Molly Beaver's honey.'

She then flopped into her chair with a deep

sigh. 'Oh dearie me,' she said 'I've no energy

at all. I can't even find the energy to sweep the

floor.'

'I'll sweep the floor for you,'

volunteered Izzy beaver 'I'll take the toad and

look after it,' said Mickey Ferret, swooping it up and taking it out to his car.

Izzy beaver began to sweep the cave floor while Peggy Squirrel gave the witch a big spoonful of Peggy's medicine.

The witch passed a duster to Milly Mole

and said, 'Don't just stand there Milly Mole,

here, take this duster and dust that shelf, but

be very careful you don't knock my precious

book of spells off.

Ron Raccoon took charge of the meal and soon he had a bowl of soup ready to serve to the witch.

'Well, I am being pampered,' she said. 'I've never had anyone wait on me before.'

'We'll come again tomorrow,' said Peggy Squirrel, 'To check up on you and to give you some more medicine, I may even bake some

cakes for you.' she added.

The witch licked her lips, she looked forward

to that, she loved Peggy Squirrel's fairy cakes.

The little creatures quickly finished all their

chores and left.

They piled into Mickey Ferret's car and he

drove them back to Brockie field, with the toad

sitting on the floor of the car.

CHAPTER TEN

When the little creatures arrived, back on the field, Ron Raccoon carefully put the little toad into the Bug Hotel.

'You are our first guest,' he said. 'So, settle in and we'll see you later.' 'You won't be on your own for long, wait and see, other little

creatures and insects will join you soon.'

The toad gave a contented croak and

snuggled down into a clump of straw.

Ron then turned to the others and said 'See

you all at the Storytelling Corner later tonight.'

And with that everyone made their way back

to their homes.

Inside her home, Peggy Squirrel started to

mix ingredients for her fairy cakes, while Ron

Raccoon organised the lighting of a fire for the

story telling time and Peggy would bake the

cakes over it while they listened to the story.

The witch was very fond of fairy cakes and

Peggy was quite willing to exchange them for

a trip in the Time Machine.

When evening arrived the little creatures all

met up on the story telling bench. Mickey

Ferret told them how he had arrived back at

the cottage and noticed that the Bug Hotel,

belonging to Lady Jane, was quite full of little

insects. While Mickey told them his tale Peggy

Squirrel placed her cake tins over the log fire

which Ron had built, and in no time, they were

baked and ready to eat. 'Can I have one

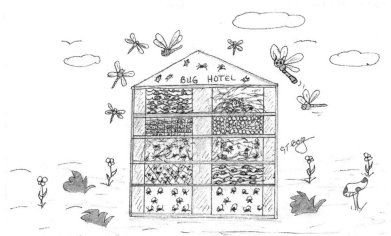

Peggy?' asked Izzy Beaver who couldn't resist

cakes, or anything sweet for that matter. At

one time Izzy had gone down to the Dock

Road in Liverpool to pick up as many pieces of

sugarcane as he could which fell off the lorries

that were loaded for delivery to the ships for export. However, he had been caught doing it and had promised never to go there again.

Suddenly they heard a croaking noise and the little toad, whom they had called Toby, suddenly appeared hopping around the bench. 'How are you settling into your new home?' asked Ron Raccoon. 'Very well thank you, and thank you for saving my life, I didn't want to be made into soup.' said Toby.

'That's ok we know how to handle the Witch of the Woods, she's not bad really, she threatens to do things but doesn't always carry out her threats, especially when we mention Peggy

Squirrel's fairy cakes,' said Ron Raccoon. 'We have toad friends who live in the sand dunes at Crosby,' said Molly Beaver,' 'But they don't look at all like you.'

'They're called Natterjack Toads, and they like water,' chipped in Betsy Beaver.

'Water, water, don't mention water to me.' 'I'm a Common Toad,' said Toby, 'And we Common Toads don't like water at all, we like to be free to hop around in open spaces like fields, though we do hibernate, just like the Natterjacks.'

'I'm going to be so comfortable in your Bug Hotel this winter.' ' I might even tell some of my friends about it as there seems to be room

for them.' said Toby Toad before he hopped

away, back inside his new home.

Suddenly they heard a mooing sound and

Daisy Cow popped her head over the hedge.

'Good evening,' she said.' 'I have some more

news for you.'

'What news?' asked Harry Hedgehog, curious

as usual. Daisy looked at Mickey Ferret but

Mickey shook his head and said. 'Sorry Daisy,

I've no mints to give you."

Daisy looked disappointed but she carried on

talking anyway, 'Farmer Jones is well again

and he's so pleased at the way Tommy Tinker,

the Odd Job man, and Fred Fettler handled

the farm in his absence, that he's going to

throw a party, and everyone's invited,' said

Daisy. 'What do you think of that?'

'I don't think he'd want us to be there,' said Ron Racoon. "But then again, on second thoughts, he does like Lady Jane because she's a great help to him in the shop, so, if he thought we were friends of hers, he might not mind us attending his celebrations.' With that thought in mind all the little creatures went off to their beds, leaving Olive Owl and Barney Bat to fly off

on their nightly hunt in the woods for midges.

CHAPTER ELEVEN

The little creatures called at the witch's cave every morning for the next two weeks. Mickey Ferret drove them to the cave in his car, as they needed to carry food, medicine and honey.

Peggy Squirrel gave the witch the special mixture she'd made together with the honey, and Izzy Beaver busied himself brushing the floor.

There was one morning, when it rained so

hard, the little creatures couldn't venture out of

their homes for almost all of the day, but,

towards evening, the rain stopped, so off they

went once more to the cave.

When they arrived, to their surprise, they

found the witch was up and about and fully

dressed. 'My spots have all gone.' she said.

'I'm completely better thanks to Peggy

Squirrel's medicine and all of your help.'

'Mirror, mirror, on the wall, tell me that I'm the

prettiest witch of all,' she chanted as she held

up her mirror.

'Now I can go to that meeting with my witchy

friends in Transylvania.' 'I haven't forgotten

that you want an adventure in my Time

Machine, so hopefully, I'll come back with a

spell to fix it.' 'I always keep my promises,' she

added. With that, she picked up her cat Trixie,

and they both zoomed out of sight, across the

sky, balancing on her broomstick.

'Well, that's that, we've accomplished our

mission which was to get the witch better, now

let's go and see what's going on at the farm,

I'm sure I heard music as we passed it on our way here,' said Ron Raccoon.

'Your right, I definitely heard music, too.' said Milly Mole. Mickey Ferret waited until they'd all climbed into his car then pedalled furiously to Farmer Jones' farm. When they arrived, they saw the barn all lit up, with hundreds of fairy lights hanging from the rafters, and they

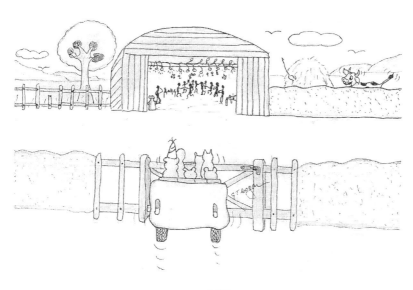

could hear the music, being played, very loudly.

'I'm hungry, let's go and get something to eat, there should be lots of food inside the barn,' said Izzy Beaver, 'Let's go quickly, it looks as though the party is already in full swing.'

'This must be the party that Daisy Cow told us about,' said Molly Beaver,

'Oh do let's hurry and go inside,' said Betsy Beaver.

Mickey Ferret parked the car at the farm gate, they all got out and made their way to the barn. When they peeped inside they could see Lady Jane and the Squire dancing together.

The farmer's wife was handing out

sandwiches. Some of the guests were looking

at a picture of Daisy Cow which now hung on

the barn wall.

'That's my painting,' said a surprised Izzy

Beaver.

'Well, by the looks of things you are now a

famous artist, Izzy, they're all admiring your

painting,' said Peggy Squirrel. Izzy was so

proud the farmer had hung his painting on the wall.

The friends all tiptoed into the barn, and were soon all tucking into apples, bananas and cream cakes. (But they all agreed the cakes were not as good as Peggy's fairy cakes.) Lady Jane spotted them as she danced by with the Squire.

'Oh there's our Mickey Ferret with his little friends,' she said, 'They look as though they're enjoying themselves.'

As they waltzed past the picture of Daisy Cow Lady Jane said, 'What a nice painting, come to think of it, some of the paints from my toy basket have disappeared, I wonder where they went. Sometimes things mysteriously disappear from our cottage and then quite suddenly, turn up again. I wonder if Mickey Ferret has anything to do with that.'

'He probably has,' said the Squire.

Much later that night, when the party was over, they all went back to Brockie Field once more, where they found that the Bug Hotel

was full of Ladybirds, insects and dragonflies.

'Isn't that just wonderful,' said Ron Racoon.

'Tomorrow, I'll ask Olive Owl to write a **- No**

Vacancies - notice and hang it on the Bug

Hotel.

Didn't we all do well?' he said, as he turned

and headed off, to his home.

Then all the little creatures made their

separate ways, back to their own homes, to

sleep and to dream about their next adventure

in the Time Machine.

'What and where would that be?'

THE END

www.facebook.com/gonzalezstories

www.izzybeaver.co.uk

Printed in Poland
by Amazon Fulfillment
Poland Sp. z o.o., Wrocław

88938620R00069